The BRAIN

Now Standing On

Platform Three

Robin Kingsland

Hodder
Children's
Books

a division of Hodder Headline plc

First published in Great Britain in 1995
by Hodder Children's Books

10   9   8   7   6   5   4   3   2   1

A Catalogue record for this book is available from the British Library

ISBN 0340 619643

Printed and bound in Great Britain by
Cox & Wyman Ltd, Reading, Berks.

Hodder Children's Books
a division of Hodder Headline plc
338 Euston Road
London NW1 3BH

CHAPTER ONE

A motorway somewhere in south-west England.

"It's twelve o'clock, and this is the news from the BBC.

Another kidnapped scientist has been found. Once again the victim reappeared early in the morning at a remote railway station. Doctor Inge Brodfrod, a world famous rocket-propulsion specialist, was found at the little station of Thridwell-cum-Hodly. Eye-witnesses say that Doctor Brodfrod was standing alone, staring vacantly into space, and refused to respond when questioned. Police confirmed this, adding that the alarm would have been raised sooner if the doctor hadn't been mistaken for a member of station staff. Meanwhile in Scotland, the international peace summit..."

Mum switched off the radio and tutted. "That's the fourth one they've found this month!" she said. "Honestly. I don't know what the world's coming to!"

"Talking of coming to," Laura said, "how much further is it to Granny...Whotsit's?"

Laura was gazing out of the car window, and getting more and more bothered. She and her mum had been driving for hours, and there seemed to be fewer and fewer signs of civilisation - the last *Happy Stuffy-face* restaurant they'd passed was an hour ago!

"She's Granny *Smith*," Mum said. "Although she's actually your great-grandmother, on your dad's side. And we should be there in another hour."

"Another HOUR!" Laura groaned. "You said she lived in the country! But you didn't say *which* country!"

Until this morning, Laura had been blissfully unaware of any lurking great-grandmothers. Then her mum, who was a film-maker, had been offered a month's work in some rainforest somewhere. At times like this, Laura usually stayed with her Auntie Anne, who was young, and fun, and insisted on being called Annie. But Annie had just had twins, so looking after Laura was out of the question. Mum had gone to one relative after the other, and they were all away, or busy, or already had people staying. Then someone had suggested Granny Smith... so here they were, driving deeper and deeper into some sort of rural twilight zone!

"Suppose this place doesn't have a cinema?" Laura said in sudden panic. "Or an ice-rink - or a computer-games centre?"

"It's called Pelsham," her mum corrected, "and you'll love it - even if it doesn't have all the things you're used to in the city. After that noise and pollution, a couple of weeks in the country will do you the world of good."

"I *love* noise and pollution," Laura protested. But Mum wasn't listening any more.

CHAPTER TWO
The car, two and a half hours later.

They passed a sign. *WELCOME TO PELSHAM*, it said. Laura looked. There was a green, and a pond, a pub and a church, and three little white cottages. They passed another sign. This one said *PLEASE VISIT AGAIN*.

"Was that *it*?" Laura asked. "It was minute!"

"I thought it was lovely," Mum said.

"And Granny Smith lives there?"

"Actually she lives just outside. She says she doesn't like the bustle of the village..."

CHAPTER THREE

Hydrangea Cottage, Pelsham.

A few minutes later, after a bumpy drive
up a rutted track, Mum stopped the car.
Laura clambered out opposite a short
row of low, red-brick lock-keepers'
cottages. Half of one cottage was
completely covered in ivy. Trailing plants
poured from baskets hanging on either
side of the door, and little lace curtains
peeped from the windows. Laura
wondered how long it would take for a
healthy ten year old to die of boredom!

"This is the one," Mum said cheerily.
She rapped on the door of Hydrangea
Cottage and waited. Nothing happened.
She peered in at the window. "Maybe
she's hard of hearing," she murmured.

"No she's not!"

Mum jumped three feet at the sudden
voice. Laura looked around. Coming out
of the garden gate at the side of the
cottage was one of the smallest old ladies

that Laura had ever seen. She had white hair, and behind her tortoiseshell spectacles, blue eyes sparkled. Everything else about her was beige - beige stockings, beige skirt, beige cardigan.

"That's all I need," Laura muttered to herself. "An old beige pensioner."

"Hello, my dears," Granny Smith piped. "Come along inside. I've got the kettle on!"

Laura and Mum perched on the edge of the little sofa, and pecked their way through a never-ending supply of cakes and sandwiches. As Mum and Granny chattered about various family members, Laura looked around. An old clock thudded away on the mantelpiece above the crackling fire. Little white doily things lay everywhere, from the backs of the armchair to the top of the old-fashioned radiogram. And from his cage, Philby the cockatoo glared down at them all.

BWRRK-K!

Laura was just looking down at the neat little pile of things next to Granny's armchair. There, kebabbed on its needles, was a roll of knitting. There were a couple of dull-looking paperbacks, a hair brush, and...what

10

was that other magazine? The one with the snazzy cover. Laura tilted her head and squinted, trying to make out the title. E..S..P..I...

Granny was not facing Laura, but without pausing for a moment in her chatter to Laura's mum, she reached round with her toe, and deftly pushed the magazine under the chair.

When Mum was leaving, Laura went out to say goodbye and whispered quietly, "Mum? What's Espion..Espi-on...*Espionage*?"

"Espionage?" Mum repeated, mystified. "It's a fancy word for spying. Why?"

"I just wondered. Granny's got a magazine about it."

Mum hooted with laughter. "You must have made a mistake, Laura. Why on earth would a little old lady have a magazine about *spying*? It probably said gardening!"

With a few warnings to behave, and a promise to send a postcard, she started the car and began the long bumpy journey to the main road.

CHAPTER FOUR

Laura had made a solemn promise to her mum that she would behave. After all, Mum had said, Granny Smith was quite old and it had been very kind of her to let Laura stay. In return, it was only fair that Laura should blah, blah, blah... So when Granny suggested that Laura go for a long walk to "get some fresh air inside her," she did as she was told. That was the first day. Then it happened again on the second day...

...and the third day...

By the time Granny shooed her out of the house for the fifth day running, Laura was getting pretty fed up. She'd had as much country air as she could take. Since she'd arrived at Granny's, she'd probably taken in more air than a bouncy castle!

On her way out, Laura walked past the kitchen window. She heard Granny talking and peeped in. What she saw made her very curious indeed...

Laura pretended to walk jauntily along to the first bend in the canal. Then, ducking into the undergrowth, she started to work back to the cottage. She got stung a couple of times, and the brambles gave her a few scratches, but Laura was determined, and in a few minutes, she was edging along the garden wall of the end cottage.

"Hello!" said a voice, very close behind her.

Laura whirled round to find - no-one!

"I'm up here!" the voice said.

Laura looked up - and found herself

staring at an upside-down grin, with freckles and a shock of red hair hanging under it.

"My glasses have fallen off," said the face. "Hand 'em up, will you?"

Her gaze travelled further up. A boy, about her own age, or possibly younger, was dangling from a tree by a long steel wire which was attached to a small metal box on his belt.

"Don't just stand there gawping," the boy said grumpily. "Give us me specs back!" He began to thump the metal box.

15

"Are you stuck?" Laura asked.

"NO!" the boy snapped.

"You look stuck to me."

"Well, I'm not. If I *wanted* to get down I'd just press this little button on the side, and slowly..."

There was a horrible grinding squeal, and the wires and the box parted company. The boy might have been badly hurt in the fall...

...if he hadn't landed on Laura.

The two helped each other up. "My name's Eric Dean Percival Potter," the boy said matter-of-factly. "But everyone calls me The Mind, 'cos I'm good with machines." He caught Laura's sly look at the broken wires, blushed and added "*some* machines!"

Laura introduced herself. Darren Dean Percival Potter lived just along from Laura's granny. He and Laura were temporary neighbours.

"Why were you up that tree?" Laura asked.

16

"I was experimenting," The Mind said. "OK, my turn. Why were you sneaking along our wall?"

Laura hesitated. Then she decided that a friend, even one who fell on you out of trees, was a good thing to have at a time like this.

"Well," she began. "It's my Granny, Mrs Smith. I think she's mad!"

"Why, what have you done?"

"Not mad *angry*," Laura groaned. "Mad *loopy*! I just caught her talking to the microwave!"

"You must have made a mistake," The Mind said. "She was probably on the phone."

"There isn't a phone in the kitchen."

"Talking to herself then. Old people do that sometimes."

"I'm telling you," Laura said firmly, "she was talking to the microwave. She pressed a button, the pinger went ping, and she talked to it! And she had a magazine the other day, all about

17

espi..eppi...epsi...Spying!"

"Hmm," The Mind knitted his brow. "I think we should do a little spying of our own."

A few minutes later, Laura and The Mind were crouching under the kitchen window. The Mind had popped into his own house and returned with a home-made periscope. He slowly lifted it until it was just above the window-sill.

"What's she doing?" Laura hissed.

"Baking," The Mind said. "Not exactly top secret stuff, is it? She's putting on some oven gloves...she's taking a tray out of the oven...she's coming towards us...she..."

"Hide!" Laura gasped.

Just in time, she pulled The Mind behind the rainwater barrel. There was a swish as the kitchen door opened, and Granny came out with a tray of scones. She disappeared round the corner. The Mind crept out of hiding.

"Come on," he said.

18

"Come on where?"

"Into the kitchen," The Mind said. "If she can talk to the microwave, then so can we!"

Laura began to argue, but The Mind was already halfway through the door. Laura followed, shutting the door behind her. She stayed to keep look-out.

The Mind turned his attention to the microwave. He twiddled a dial and pressed a button. The 'ping!' was so loud that they both ducked, but nothing else happened.

"Maybe there's another button," Laura said.

Suddenly there was a noise from the living room. Granny's cockatoo, Philby, was getting restless.

"Bwaaark!" he squawked. "Restricted access. No unauthorised personnel. Hands off, hands off! Bwwaark-k-k!"

"Quick!" The Mind hissed. "Shut him up or she'll hear him!"

Laura rushed in and threw a cover

over Philby's cage. The bird fell into a sulky silence. By the time Laura went back into the kitchen, The Mind had pulled the machine away from the wall and was examining the back panel. "Wow!" he breathed. "Wow,wowowwow!" He pressed another switch. Laura's mouth dropped open."Look!" she gasped. Words were appearing on the microwave door:

This is
G.L.A.D.Y.S
Please enter G.R.A.N.
Access code...

"Ours never does that!" Laura murmured.
"This is no microwave," The Mind announced. "It's some kind of disguised computer terminal!"

Then a weird thing happened. A red rabbit-shaped jelly mould on the wall began to flash.

"Aren't you going to pick that up?" said The Mind.

"No!"

"Why not? Scared!?"

"NO!" Laura reached for the mould, then she hesitated. She took a step back. She squared her shoulders, cleared her throat, and lifted the scarlet bunny from the wall.

"Peabody!" barked a no-nonsense handlebar-moustache of a voice.

"Peabody? Is that you?"

"Peabody?" Laura was confused. "Who's Peabody?"

"I am!" said a stern voice from the kitchen door. Laura and The Mind whirled round. Granny Smith stood silhouetted in the kitchen doorway. She strode across the kitchen, switched off the microwave and grabbed the jelly-mould from Laura's stunned fingers.

"Go into the front room," she commanded, "and don't come in until I call you!"

For what seemed like forever, Laura and The Mind sat in silence. Neither of them could think of anything to say. Then Granny called them into the garden. The tray of scones lay on an ornamental table. Reaching behind a flowerpot, Granny brought out a couple of rusty old helmets and thrust them at the children. "You'll need these," she said.

Laura and The Mind stared at each other. What was the old fruit bat going to do to them?

Nothing. Instead, she began to take the scones, and lob them, one by one, in long slow arcs up the garden.

Laura leaned across to The Mind and whispered, "This is what she was doing earlier. Weird or what!"

Finally, the old lady spoke. "By rights, I should be telling you off," she said, "but I suppose I can't blame you for being curious. Now, how much do you know?"

Laura and The Mind looked at each other again. The Mind decided to play dumb, "I know about materials that float," he said. "We did that last term. And I know some French - Je m'appel Darren.

And I know - OW!"

"There's no point in lying," said Laura. She told Granny everything they had heard and seen, while the old lady continued to lob scones up the garden.

When Laura had finished, Granny stopped and muttered "I warned them. I said this would happen." Then, hurling another scone, she said, "G.L.A.D.Y.S - the computer, helps me with my work, my dears. Sometimes I need information in a hurry, you see."

"What do you do?" Laura asked.

Granny hesitated. "Have you ever heard of G.R.A.N., dear?"

The two children shook their heads. Granny explained. "The letters stand for Global Retired Agents Network. It's a branch of MI5. I work for them. O. A. Peabody is my codename."

The Mind's mouth fell open. "You mean...you're a spy? Like James Bond?"

"Exactly. In fact, I trained him! Of course I was younger then!"

Laura and The Mind stared at each other. Granny threw another scone, then turned and looked hard at the two of them. "You don't believe me, do you?" she said.

"Well, since you ask..." Laura began.

With perfect timing, and an ear-splitting boom, the scone exploded. A fountain of turf and soil flew into the air, half a gnome thudded into the fence, a mushroom cloud of white smoke rose, and dirt and weeds rained down on the cowering heads of Laura and The Mind.

"Bingo!" said Granny Smith. "Now, you were saying?"

"We were saying," Laura continued. "We

were saying, of *course* we believe you!"

"Good," said Peabody. "Because I've just been called to G.R.A.N. Headquarters and you two are going to have to come with me!"

Peabody got changed. The flowery apron and frilly blouse went. Now, she was wearing a loose track-suit. She locked the cottage and led the children down the lane to a small barn. They stepped through the door into a cool, dusty darkness. "This is where I keep the car," Granny explained, feeling around for the light switch.

"I wonder what it's called?" muttered The Mind. "The Granny Mobile? The Wrinkly Ranger? Old Reliable?"

Granny found the switch. Laura and The Mind gasped as powerful lights suddenly flashed onto Granny's transportation.

"You call it what you like, dear," she said, sliding into the driving seat.
"I call it a Porsche 6.5 Turbo!"

CHAPTER FIVE

"Wow," The Mind kept saying, as they glided at incredible speeds through the countryside. "Wow, wow, wow!" He reached for a button. "What does this do?"

"Don't fiddle, dear," Peabody commanded. "You might hit the ejector seat button."

The Mind jumped back, white-faced. Laura leant over to Granny. "Is there really an ejector seat?" she whispered.

"Of course not," Granny winked, "but it'll keep The Mind's fingers from mucking up my upholstery, won't it?"

It was true. For the rest of the journey, The Mind sat on his hands, and smiled nervously.

"Here we are!" said Peabody. She pulled the car into a long gravel drive. At the end stood a vast white house. Granny drove right up to the wide front steps and brought the car to a scrunching halt.

Everybody got out. *SUNNYSIDE RETIREMENT HOME*, a sign said. The Mind turned to Laura.

"I thought we were going to G.R.A.N. Headquarters?" he said.

"This is G.R.A.N Headquarters!" Peabody replied.

"But it says - "

"What did you expect it to say? *SECRET AGENT HEADQUARTERS, PLEASE COME IN AND LOOK AROUND?*"

They passed through huge panelled doors to find themselves in a world of polished wood, polished floors, thick rugs, and leather armchairs. Every voice murmured and every footstep rang.

A nurse in dark glasses rose from

behind a table to greet them, "Hello, Peabody. Go straight through. He's expecting you." She looked at The Mind and raised one eyebrow. "All of you," she sighed.

She reached behind her, and pressed a secret button in one of the wooden panels. With a purr, the wall slid away. Laura and The Mind found themselves in a long wide room.

Apart from the few chairs, a big map and a tall man with an eye-patch, there was very little furniture.

"Laura, The Mind," Granny said. "I'd like you to meet the Major!"

The Major shook their hands until their teeth rattled.

"Look, Peabody," the Major said. "I'll get straight to the point. In the past three months, at least twelve top scientists have disappeared while working on secret government projects. Experts in rocket propulsion, psychology, brain surgery. The list is endless..."

"And you want me to find them, dear?" Granny asked.

"That's the strange thing, Peabody," the Major said. "Each one turns up again a few days after going walkies. Usually at some remote rural railway station."

"Try saying that ten times fast!" The Mind muttered.

"Shhhh!" Laura hissed.

"Trouble is," the Major went on, "these poor blighters have no idea where they've been, or what's happened to them. It's as if their memories have been wiped!"

"I see," Granny stood up. "This

30

sounds like the work of P.A.N.I.C.!"

"My thoughts exactly!" the Major agreed.

"Panic? What's that?" The Mind asked.

"Don't you know anything?" Laura sneered. Then she realised that she had no idea either.

"P.A.N.I.C." Granny explained, "stands for Programmed Action to Nurture International Chaos. The leader is an evil genius called Dr Lazlo Proonefinger. He wants to use the organisation to take over the world!"

"I won't deny it, Peabody," the Major said, "we're worried. We need to get to the bottom of this business!"

Granny walked over to the map on the wall. Scattered across it were little flag pins. "Are these the stations where the scientists have been found?"

"Yes," said the Major. "As you can see, they're spread over a huge area."

Granny stared up at the map for a few minutes. Her fingertips drummed together, her eyes narrowed, a thoughtful frown settled on her face. Suddenly she peered at a little speck roughly in the middle of all the flags. "What's this, my dear?" she asked. The Major bent down to try and read the tiny letters.

"Wildwoods," he muttered. "Wildwoods? No idea. Can't help you. Sorry, Peabody."

"I know what it is!" It was The Mind.

Everyone turned to stare at him.

"I do know what Wildwoods is!" he said. "It's an Adventure Park! You know - rides, stalls, adventure playgrounds, ridiculously expensive hot-dogs, that sort of thing! It's been going for years."

Suddenly Laura twigged. Of course. Wildwoods - World of Thrills. She'd seen it advertised on the telly. It had been built by a millionaire miniature railway nut, Sir Gilpin Stoak-Boyler, in the grounds of his stately home. In the ads, he chugged across the screen on a tiny train saying "It's Weelly Wild at Wildwoods!"

"Interesting," said the Major. "I wonder if there's a connection. Peabody?"

Peabody turned to the children. "How would you like a day at Wildwoods, my dears?"

"You bet!" said Laura. "When?"

"Would tomorrow be a good day?" asked her granny.

33

CHAPTER SIX

They went to Wildwoods by train, as
Peabody decided the car would attract
too much attention. As it was, nobody
noticed the little white-haired old lady
buying her tickets and taking two
children into the Wildwoods World of
Thrills!

The Mind was right. Wildwoods had
been open for years - and it showed.
Everything they went on was a little bit
shabby. Still, Laura and The Mind had a

great morning. They tried everything - the Loop, the Twister, the ghost train, the river boat, and Dinosaur Island. Laura particularly liked the Klondike Miniature Railway, which ran through a scaled-down model of a gold-rush town, then out around all the mines.

"Can we go round again?" Laura yelled as soon as they got off. But Peabody was lost in thought.

"I wanna go on the Helter Skelter!" The Mind announced.

"There isn't one," said Laura.

"Yes there is," The Mind retorted. "Back there. I saw it from the train." He led them back along a chipped-bark path and pointed. He was right. There was a Helter Skelter. A tall fat one, with orange and yellow stripes. The trouble was that when they got there, it was covered in scaffolding, with men in boilersuits working on it. There was a seven foot fence around it, a big sign saying 'Closed for Repairs', and a whole

gang of security men standing by the fence. They were all huge, with tree-trunk legs and weightlifter's arms and foreheads so low you could have landed aeroplanes on them.

36

"The gorilla brothers!" Laura remarked.
The Mind moaned, "Just our luck!"

"Never mind, dear," Granny said. "Tell
you what. I'll take you for something to
eat and then you can go to Dinosaur
Island again." The children cheered, and
they set off towards the Klondyke Cafe.
The Mind cast a miserable glance back at
the Helter Skelter.

"Closed for repairs?" he muttered to
himself. "It looks brand new to me!"

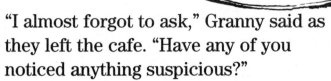

CHAPTER SEVEN

"I almost forgot to ask," Granny said as they left the cafe. "Have any of you noticed anything suspicious?"

"Yeah," The Mind said. "That burger. It tasted of old socks!"

"What about you, Gran?" Laura asked, ignoring him. "Have you seen anything?"

"I'm not sure," said Granny. "Maybe." The children waited, but since it was obvious that Granny wasn't going to say any more just yet, they started off back to Dinosaur Island.

Suddenly, Laura stopped. "Hang on a minute, Gran," she said. "You haven't been on anything yet!"

It was true. Granny had simply waited in the queues for each ride with the children, then met them at the exits when they came out. At first she protested that she didn't mind, but under questioning, she admitted to a slight temptation.

"I noticed a rifle range back there,"

she said. "I wouldn't mind having a go at that!"

The children took her by the hand and dragged her off to find the fake log cabin that housed the OK Corral rifle range.

"There!" said The Mind. "You get ten shots - and if you get eight bulls' eyes, you win a prize!"

Ten minutes later, Laura and The Mind had a prize each. On top of that, a small crowd of tiny admirers had formed, and half of them had prizes too. Granny was scoring perfect tens  every time. In the end, the stall-holder asked Granny to move on.

"Sorry, love," he said, "but if you stay here much longer, I'll have no prizes left!"

"That was incredible," said The Mind, as they walked away.

Granny leaned down and whispered. "Don't tell anyone, but I was MI5 champion during the war!"

"I only wish I'd brought my camera," marvelled Laura.

Laura didn't know it, but Granny's sharp-shooting had already been captured on camera - *video* camera. And in a room of Wildwood House itself, at the centre of the Park, two people were watching the tapes very closely indeed. One was Sir Gilpin Stoak-Boyler, owner of Wildwoods.

The other was a huge jelly of a man with glasses as thick as bottle bottoms. His

name? Doctor Lazlo Proonefinger - head
of the international crime organisation
known as PANIC!

Proonefinger turned to a white-coated
assistant. "That woman," he said. "The
white-haired one with the children..."

"Yes, Doctor Proonefinger?"

"Have her followed. I wish to know
where she goes."

"Yes Doctor Proonefinger!"

"And double the guard on the house."

The white-coated man picked up a
telephone, and began to send out his
master's orders. Proonefinger peered at
the screen, and smiled. "So, O. A.
Peabody," he murmured. "We meet again.
But not, I assure you, for long." And he
laughed a wicked, humourless laugh...

Peabody had booked a room in a little
bed and breakfast hotel, run by a very
friendly couple, Mr and Mrs Trubshaw.
The children bathed and had some
supper. Then Peabody got up from her

chair. "Bed-time!" she announced.

"OK, Granny," Laura said. "Goodnight!"

"Not my bedtime, silly. Yours!"

Laura and The Mind exploded into protests. It was only half-past seven, they said, they were always allowed to stay up later at home, they said. Just a few more minutes, they said.

"All right..." said Peabody at last. "You can stay up until I get back."

"Back? Back from where? You've only just come in!" The Mind said.

"I know," said Peabody, "and now, I need to pop out again!" And she closed the door of her bedroom.

"What shall we do?" Laura said. "There's nothing on the telly!"

"I could thrash you at Hangman!" offered The Mind.

"Ha! I'd like to see you try!"

They dug out some paper and settled themselves on the floor. But they didn't have a pen between them. The Mind volunteered to look inside Peabody's handbag. Rummaging through the clutter in its depths, he pulled out a slender gold biro. "This should do it!" he said. But there was no button to get the nib to come out.

"'S funny..." he muttered, and began twisting and pulling and shaking the pen.

In the space of a few short seconds, several things happened. First, Peabody came out of the room and saw The Mind with her pen. She leapt at him, yelling. At the same time, The Mind, who was squinting down the barrel of the pen to see if the nib was jammed, tentatively squeezed the clip mechanism. With a flying dive, Peabody knocked the pen away - as a searing orange beam spat across the room. There was a hissing crackling noise, and a smell of burning, and suddenly a plate-sized hole

PFFFFTTZZTT!

appeared in the wall.

The Mind was seriously alarmed. He shook the pen again to try to stop the beam. The scorching light beam scythed around the room. Within seconds, flowers were decapitated, curtains shortened, and a three-piece suite converted into a six pieces.

"Put it down!" Granny yelled. "Just DROP IT!"

The Mind flung the pen away. The beam retracted. Faint wisps of smoke hung in the air. The room smelled like a bonfire party. A deathly hush fell.

"That was my laser cutter pen!" said Peabody at last.

"No kidding!" breathed The Mind, wiping sweat from his brow.

down and picked the  pen off the carpet. Peabody reached She held it up, and blew the last traces of smoke from the nib.

"This, along with most of the other stuff I carry, is G.R.A.N. property," she said sternly. "Never...ever...and I mean *EVER*...use stuff from my bag without asking! Is that clearly understood?"

Laura and the Mind dropped their heads in shame. It was only now that all the excitement was over, that they noticed what Peabody was wearing. The cardigan was gone, along with the skirt, the scarf, and the sensible shoes. Instead, Peabody was dressed head to toe in camouflage - camouflage jacket, camouflage trousers, camouflage hat, the lot. On her face were streaks of green and brown paint, and on her feet were black, rubber-soled shoes.

"I thought you were just 'popping out'?" Laura gasped. "I am," Peabody said simply. "I want to have another look around Wildwoods while no one else is around!" Heaving the window open, Peabody climbed onto the ledge as if it were the most natural thing in the world to leave a room by the drainpipe. "Now if there's an emergency, just pick up the phone, and call Mrs Trubshaw downstairs, all right? Otherwise I'll see you at around nine. And then you really are going to bed!" Grabbing her handbag, O. A. Peabody dropped silently, then disappeared into the twilight.

"Be careful, Granny," Laura said quietly.

46

Laura's plan was to stay up until Peabody returned, but she just couldn't keep her eyes open. Next thing she knew, it was pitch dark outside and she was lying uncomfortably on what was left of the sofa. The Mind was curled up in the unburned half of the armchair. Laura looked at the clock. Granny should have been back by now. She stretched, walked across the room and tapped quietly on the bedroom door.

"Granny?"
There was no answer."Oh, Granny? How did it go?" No answer. Laura started to get a cold feeling in her stomach.

"Granny?" Still nothing. Something must be wrong. Laura pushed the door wide open. The room was empty!

Laura ran back and shook The Mind awake.

"Wass going on?" he grumbled, still half-asleep.

"Gonny's gran!" Laura gabbled. "I mean, Granny's gone! We must get help,

47

contact the Major, call the police! We
must do something! Anything!!"

"About what, my dears?"
At Peabody's voice, Laura turned so fast
that she nearly tripped over the bed.
"What's the problem?" the old lady asked
again, as she
clambered
through the
window.

"She thought
you'd been
kidnapped!" the
Mind said.

"Sneak!"
Laura sneered.

"So Mrs P. What did you find out?"

"My dears, my dears! Don't rush me!"
Peabody protested. "Let me get these
clothes changed and have a bath, and I'll
tell you all about it."

CHAPTER EIGHT

Doctor Proonefinger toyed with a pencil, trying to control his rage. He had just found out a section of the Theme Park fence had been damaged.

"We fink there's been an intruder, Boss," said the guard.

The pencil snapped, splinters flew across the room. "*Of course there's been an intruder*!" Proonefinger screeched.

"Peabody!" he growled though gritted teeth. "It has to be Peabody!! She will ruin everything!" He turned to Sir Gilpin, who shifted uneasily. "I hold you responsible for this, Stoak-Boyler!" he snarled. "You assured me that your men could handle security. Well, as usual, it seems I have to do everything!" He turned to the technician beside him. "I think the time has come to give O. A. Peabody a little telephone call, hmm? Make the necessary arrangements!" And barging past Stoak-Boyler, he wobbled irritably out of the room.

Peabody had changed back into her usual clothes. "Now then, my dears. What was it you wanted to know?"

"What happened last night?" Laura urged. "Tell us what you saw."

"Well," Peabody began, "I had a good look round, and it's all very interesting. Especially that Helter Skelter. One thing's for sure. Doctor Proonefinger is behind everything..." her voice tailed off as she thought about the evil doctor.

"Granny?" The Mind tugged her arm,

"Granny! Have you solved the mystery? The disappearing scientists?"

"What? Oh, yes dear. That is, I know *why* they kidnap these scientists, and I've a feeling I know *how* it's done. You see -"

Frrrrrring frring! Frrrrrring frring!

"Excuse me a moment, my dears," Peabody said. She picked up the telephone. "Hello? Is that you, Mrs Trubshaw?" Laura had always been taught that it's rude to listen to other people's conversations. She went to brush her teeth. Meanwhile The Mind started playing idly with the TV remote.

As she came out of the bathroom, Laura heard the telephone receiver click.

"Who was it, Granny?" she asked.

To her utter astonishment, Peabody walked straight past her, towards the door.

"Granny?" Laura said. "What's wrong?"

There was no reply. Laura ran after her relative and overtook her in the corridor. "Gran? Is anything the matt-ooof!" She went sprawling, as Peabody swept her aside, eyes fixed on the stairs ahead. It was as if she didn't even see Laura, as if she didn't see anything in her way. As if...

Laura ran back to the room, and pulled The Mind out of the armchair. "Granny's been hypnotised!" she yelled. "Get some shoes on. We have to follow her."

They threw their things on and scrambled out into the corridor. The Mind suddenly slid to a halt, turned and ran back into the room.

"What are you doing?!" Laura hissed. "Hurry up!"

The Mind reappeared, holding Peabody's handbag aloft. "We might need this. It's got some of her gadgets in it!"

"But she said - "

"I know what she said. But this is an emergency!"

They scrambled along the corridor and down the stairs. At the reception, there was no sign of Peabody. The Mind stepped forward.

"I'll ask. They're bound to have seen ıeErrrk!" He winced as Laura yanked him ›ut of sight behind a droopy rubber-plant.

"Have you seen who's on reception?" The Mind looked.

Instead of nice, fat, friendly Mrs Trubshaw, a bunch of great hulking figures paced about in the little room ›ehind the desk.

"The gorilla brothers!" The Mind ›reathed. The guards were going through

all the desk drawers, scattering papers.
They looked bored and bad-tempered.
One was looking through the hotel guest
book.

"Here we are," he said suddenly.
"Room 11. Come on."

"That's our room!" The Mind
whimpered.

"The back way!" Laura ordered.
"Quick!"

They stumbled out the back door, ran
through a little car park and headed for
the main road, but just as they reached it
they heard shouts behind them.

"Oi! You kids!!" It was the gorilla
brothers. "*RUN*!" Laura yelled.

54

CHAPTER NINE

They ran - down the road and into the
crowds shuffling through the gates of
Wildwoods. Laura and The Mind dived
under and round and through legs,
chased by shouts of "Oi!" and "Mind out!"
and "Who you shovin?" At last they lost
their pursuers in the crowd.

"At least we know how they kidnap
the scientists," Laura said.

The Mind didn't understand.

"Isn't it obvious? Hypnosis by
telephone! They pick a scientist, phone
them up, play some noise to them, and
bingo! '*At your command, oh master*!'
Now we have to find Granny!"

"Look!" The Mind hissed.

The little grey-haired figure was
taking a seat on the miniature railway.
She was the only passenger. A family

55

started to step through the turnstile to join her, but the ticket collector held up his hand. "Sorry, kids," he said firmly. "Private ride!"

Laura and The Mind watched helplessly, as the train started up and began to chug away.

Laura and The Mind ran towards the line, desperate to follow the train.

"This way!" Laura called. "It goes around in a big loop, remember?"

They crashed through the undergrowth, trying to keep Peabody in sight. It wasn't easy. The train kept disappearing behind trees. At one point, they thought they'd lost it altogether. Then The Mind held up his hand.

"Listen!" he whispered. For a second, Laura could hear nothing. Then she heard a rumble coming from over the top of a grassy bank. They scrambled up...
just in time to see Peabody's truck disappear into a tunnel mouth.

"I don't remember this!" Laura said.

"It's a secret siding," The Mind said. "Look, the rails are hidden!" He was right. The train tracks had been cunningly covered up. If they hadn't seen it, there would have been nothing to show that the miniature train had come by.

The Mind climbed over the side and dropped the short distance to the tunnel mouth.

"Can you see anything?" Laura asked.

"Nothing. It's pitch dark down here." He reached into Peabody's handbag. "Maybe she's got a....Ah! Here we are. A torch." He pressed a button. With a snap, a deadly-looking circular blade sprung out, whining as it spun. The Mind pressed another button. The blade stopped and snapped back. Instead, a thick red smokescreen began to gush from holes around the torch head. Another button, and the smoke stopped, but now, with a series of blinding flashes, the torch began to take photographs. The Mind flung the torch back into the bag, snarling.

"Flippin' spies!" he cried. "Hasn't your gran got *anything* that does what it's supposed to?" He looked up at Laura. "I'm going in, just a little way. I'll find out where it goes, and come back and tell you."

Feeling his way along the wall, The Mind edged deeper and deeper into the tunnel. For the first few yards, it was bare rock, cold and clammy to the touch. Then he felt a new surface. The tunnel seemed to stop in a solid steel plate.

The Mind leaned against the wall to think. He'd seen the train go in, and it must have gone somewhere! So this steel plate had to be some kind of door. He felt about for a handle. There wasn't one. Instead, there was some sort of metal box with buttons like a telephone keypad. It had to be some sort of coded electronic lock!

Up on the bank, Laura was getting impatient. The Mind had been down in that tunnel for ten minutes already.

"Come on, come on," she muttered.

Peabody was in danger. They didn't have time to waste. Besides, it had gone dark all of a sudden, and Laura didn't want to get caught in a thunderstorm.

She looked up. But it wasn't a storm - it was four burly gorilla guards towering over her.

"What," said the burliest one menacingly, "have we got 'ere?"

Seconds later, The Mind emerged from the tunnel. "There's a metal door down here," he said, "but I think we can-"

His voice died away. Something was wrong. Scrambling to the top of the bank, he saw trampled grass. A little further off, he could see Laura's baseball cap.

"Oh no!" The Mind said. He turned and ran back down into the tunnel.

CHAPTER TEN

The Mind stopped at the steel door and tried to gather his thoughts. The way he saw it, he had three choices: one - to go back, find help, and leave all this to the police. Two - to go back, find a real torch, and then reprogramme the door switch to a new code that he could use.

And what about choice three? That was sitting temptingly in The Mind's hand, in the shape of Peabody's little gold pen...

"OK," he said to himself, holding the pen in outstretched hands. "Just point the pencil and press – "

A searing, crackling whiplash of red-orange light shot from the end of the pencil. In the blazing lurid light, smoke filled the air, and a burning smell that stung The Mind's nostrils. He squinted as the box sparked once, twice, three times. Then it blew into a thousand pieces. The door slid open, to reveal a brightly lit, brick-lined passage. The Mind whistled quietly to himself, then picked up Granny's bag and crept in...

CHAPTER ELEVEN

Laura's feet had barely touched the ground. In a matter of minutes, she had been bundled through a back door of Wildwoods House, and frog-marched along a maze of corridors until she reached the foot of a short, carpeted staircase, leading to an imposing panelled door. Laura hesitated.

"Go on!" ordered the head gorilla, prodding her with a podgy finger. Laura reluctantly padded up the stairs, as the door sighed, and slid open.

She found herself in a sumptuous room. Amber light poured through the windows, falling on rich furniture, wooden panelled walls and crystal chandeliers. You could have laid a netball court on the floor and still had room round the edges. It was huge.

Only one thing seemed out of place. The pictures. Instead of the portraits and landscapes and posh oil paintings that you might expect, each frame on the wall contained a photo of Sir Gilpin Stoak-Boyler sitting astride one of his miniature railway locomotives. There must have been twenty around the room, at least.

Suddenly, the doors at the end of the room burst open and a troupe of guards jogged in, swinging this way and that to check that no-one was lurking in corners. These were nothing like the gorilla brothers. These guards looked highly trained, heavily armed, and very mean. Wearing silver-grey boilersuits with heavy, padded body-armour on top, each carried a laser gun. It was impossible to see any faces through the dark glass visors. They took up positions round the room, then signalled back through the door.

Two men strode in. The first one Laura recognised instantly. It was Sir Gilpin Stoak-Boyler himself. He still had on the same train driver's cap he wore in all the photos. As he came in, he nodded at Laura, and gave her a nervous smile.

But Laura wasn't watching Stoak-Boyler. Her attention had shifted to the other man, a great, bloated, waddling figure, who seemed to ripple as he moved, like a huge bald walrus. He looked Laura up and down, then turned to the gorilla squad.

"There was a boy, too," he snapped. "Where is he?"

The guards shifted uneasily and shrugged.

"Well, don't just *stand there*!" the blubberman roared. *"GO BACK OUT THERE AND FIND HIM!"*

Half the guards fell over in eagerness to get out of the door - not to find The Mind, but to get away from their furious leader! In the confusion, Laura tried to sneak out too, but she was hauled back by one of the gorilla brothers.

"Try that again and you're *geography*!" he said, his voice dripping with threat.

"Don't you mean 'Do that again and you're history'?" Laura corrected.

The gorilla knitted his chunky brows and thought long and hard. "Er... that too!" he said finally.

"So," the walrus-man said, "this is the little girl who's been poking her nose where it doesn't concern her?"

"Who are you?" Laura asked defiantly.

One of the gorillas nudged her hard. "You're not allowed to know his name - is she, Doctor Proonefinger?" The guard quailed as the fat man glared at him.

"Sorry Doctor Proo- I mean, sir," he grovelled.

"So, you're Doctor Proonefinger," Laura said. "I've heard about you."

"All bad, I hope," Proonefinger said silkily. "Now tell me, where is your little friend?"

Laura played for time. "I don't know what you're talking about."

Proonefinger appeared unconcerned. "Very well," he said. "You can tell me what you know about O. A. Peabody's mission, instead."

Laura stuck out her chin, and stood defiant and tight-lipped. Proonefinger shrugged. "No matter," he sighed. "She's too late to stop me anyway!"

Laura rushed at him. "If you've hurt my granny, you slimy sleazebucket..!"

"Ah, so she's your grandmother," Proonefinger said. He smiled evilly.

"She is quite safe, my dear." It was Stoak-Boyler who spoke. He had a quiet voice. Nervous, but kind. "Do tell her, Proonefinger."

Proonefinger looked furious, but he nodded. "Yes, she's safe - for the time being. And she will remain so, as long as you tell me where your other little friend is. It would save us all so much trouble!"

"Drop dead, Proonefinger!"

Proonefinger went red. His blubbery face quivered.  Then he exploded. "How dare you speak to me like that. I, the next ruler of the world! I, who have created...*THIS*!"

He stabbed a podgy finger at a button. Part of the wall slid away, to reveal a gigantic screen showing a vast circular cavern. Metal stairways criss-crossed the walls, leading up to metal galleries that clattered constantly as men and women clanked up and down. Electric buggies scooted across the chamber floors.

The people in the chamber divided into two types: technicians in white coats, and Proonefinger's guards in their silver boilersuits. The White-coats walked round briskly, carrying clipboards, or intricate pieces of electrical gadgetry. The Boilersuits were different. They just stood around, holding those strange-looking ray guns and watching everything through their black visors.

But it was the middle of the chamber that caught Laura's attention. For, standing there, in the centre of everything, with steam floating gently from various valves, was a red and yellow rocket. At least, the lower half of one. The top half was somewhere high up in the darkness above the bright white lights that lit the chamber.

It *was* the same colour as the Helter

Skelter, Laura noticed. She looked closer. It *was* the Helter Skelter.

That's why it had been so heavily guarded. It wasn't being repaired at all. It was the top section of Proonefinger's rocket.

"The Proonefinger X1," the fat doctor crowed. "Designed by some of the best brains in the world, though they themselves will never know it."

"Because you hypnotised them by phone?" Laura stated.

"Precisely. They came here under hypnosis, worked under hypnosis, and were left scattered around the country, each blissfully unaware of their small role in my master plan!"

Laura wrinkled her lip. "So you've got a rocket," she said coolly. "So what?"

Proonefinger seethed, barely keeping the lid on his temper. "In a few short hours," he spluttered, "that rocket will be launched into orbit around the earth. Inside is the most powerful Hypnotic Control Ray known to mankind. Once it is launched, activated, and pointed at the earth, every living creature on this planet will be *in my power*!"

Laura fell silent. She had a horrible feeling that Proonefinger was telling the truth.

"But I'm being unforgivably rude!" Proonefinger said. "You must be missing your grandmother. Fear not! I will see to it that you are never separated again - *EVER*!" He snapped his fingers and one of his special guards jumped to attention. "Take the girl to Peabody. Put them both in the rocket!"

"But Proonefinger!" Sir Gilpin Stoak-Boyler cried. "You can't launch with them inside. They'll die!"

"Yes," Proonefinger agreed. "Eventually."

"But you promised me that no-one would be hurt!"

"Did I?" Proonefinger looked surprised. "How very foolish of me." He turned to the guard again, "Take her away!"

"NO!" Suddenly Stoak-Boyler's voice rang with authority. "I cannot allow it. Dominating the world is one thing, but hurting old ladies and children...I will not stand here and let you do this!"

"You're right. You won't," said Proonefinger. *Take him too*!"

"You'll never get away with this," Laura said, as they were bundled out.

"On the contrary, child," Proonefinger hissed. "I already have!"

CHAPTER TWELVE

"I'm sorry. So very sorry," Stoak-Boyler whispered, as he, Laura and a couple of guards descended in a lift.

"That man is a grade one nut-case!!" Laura whispered. "How on earth did you get tangled up with him?"

"I...I was broke," Stoak-Boyler whimpered. "The theme park was losing money, and I thought I'd have to sell the whole estate. Proonefinger offered me millions, as well as..." He tailed off.

"As well as what?" Laura whispered.

Stoak-Boyler's face went crimson. "Proonefinger said that when he ruled the world - I could be in charge of all the railways."

"I see," Laura nodded. "You let him take over so that you could have the biggest train set in history!"

Stoak-Boyler nodded, head drooping, shame-faced.

The lift stopped with a soft jolt.

Stepping out, Laura and Stoak-Boyler found themselves in a brightly-lit tunnel that curved away, with other tunnels feeding into it. Various White-coats and Boilersuits walked briskly to and fro.

From one of the side tunnels, Laura heard a high, milk-float hum. Moments later a long electric truck snaked into view. It was about six compartments long, with one of Proonefinger's faceless Boilersuits at the controls. Just as it was passing, Laura's guard signalled it to stop. He barked instructions, pointing to his prisoners. The driver nodded eagerly. Laura and Stoak-Boyler, urged on by a shove from the guards, clambered in behind him. The guards tried to sit on either side, but the driver shook his head, and pointed to the coach behind. Shrugging, the guards sloped back and climbed on board.

The driver pushed a button. The truck lurched off, then stopped so suddenly that everyone was thrown forward.

73

Almost immediately it started again, kangarooing violently as it headed off down the tunnel.

"Oof! He must be a learner," Laura muttered, as the truck slowly came under control. She looked behind to see how the guards were.

They had gone. With all that stop-start nonsense, the rear trucks had become dislodged. She could just see the guards in the distance shaking their fists as the truck turned into a side tunnel. Laura leaned over to Stoak-Boyler. "We've lost the other guards," she whispered. "Let's jump the driver!"

"Don't you dare!" said the driver, turning round.

"How did *you* get here?" Laura exclaimed.

"Never mind that now!" The Mind said, throwing off his visor hood. "Phew! It's hot in those things! Now, we have to move fast. They'll soon work out what's happened and raise the alarm. Before they do that, we have to rescue your gran!"

"Oh, good," Laura sighed. "Then you know where she is?"

"No. I thought you would!"

"So neither of us knows. Great!"

"Excuse me for interrupting," Stoak-Boyler said. "But I can take you to her."

Pulling his visor hood back on, The Mind started the truck. They whirred through the maze of tunnels, directed by Stoak-Boyler.

"What *is* this place?" asked Laura, in amazement.

"One of my ancestors built it," said Stoak-Boyler. "Spent practically all his time and money building miles of tunnels under the house. Poor chap was mad as a hatter. We used some of the tunnels for the miniature railway, but Proonefinger has taken over the rest for this rocket project. Now, here we are."

They had emerged into the main cavern that Laura had seen earlier. It looked even bigger in real life. Along one side of the chamber, rows of rubber tracked tanks were lined up, with terrifying ray-guns mounted on them.

Laura shuddered. Boilersuits and White-coats scurried about, too busy to notice the newcomers. High above, a huge clock counted backwards. ZERO MINUS NINE, it said.

"Less than ten minutes to launch!" The Mind whispered. "We'd better hurry."

"The cages are over there," Stoak-Boyler said, pointing. Laura tapped the Mind on the shoulder.

"Pull in," she ordered, nodding at a pile of fuel cylinders.

Taking care to stay in the shadows, the little group crept towards the cages.

76

Sure enough, Peabody was in there, along with the Trubshaws from the bed and breakfast and a couple of kidnapped scientists. More of a problem were the two gorillas who stood in front of the cage, bellies straining their uniform buttons.

"What do we do about them?" The Mind groaned.

"Leave them to me," Sir Gilpin said. "They probably don't know I've been sacked yet!"

Bold as brass, he walked up to the guards. "I wouldn't like to be in your shoes," he said.

"Woss wrong wiv my shoes?" said the first guard, staring at his feet.

"Nothing. I just meant that Proonefinger wants to see you. And he doesn't look very happy."

The two gorillas gulped. "We haven't done nuffin'!" But they scuttled off rapidly.

Laura and The Mind rushed out of hiding. As soon as she saw them,

Peabody leaped up!

"Oh, my dears!" she cried. "I've been so worried about you." Then she glared suspiciously at Stoak-Boyler.

"It's OK, Gran," Laura said. "He's on our side - now!"

"I'm afraid I've got you all into terrible danger," worried Peabody. "And I'm not sure how to get you out of it. If only I had my bag of tricks."

"You mean this one, Mrs P?" The Mind said, drawing the familiar handbag from the great folds of his boilersuit. Peabody upturned the bag, and a cascade of brushes, make-up, mints, pens and tissues fell to the floor.

"Good boy!" Granny exclaimed, and began to root though the pile. "Ah...no laser pen...missile-launcher lipstick. They must have dropped out... Never mind. It'll just have to be these – "

Laura, Stoak-Boyler and The Mind stared at each other in amazement, as Granny pulled a gleaming set of dentures from the bag.

"There's a train or something that goes past every couple of minutes," she said, as she clamped the gnashers on to the lock. "The noise should help. Now, get behind those barrels."

A clattering began somewhere outside - faint, but getting nearer every moment.

CLAKATA
CLAKATA
CLAKATA
CLAKATA
CLAKATA!

"Good!" Granny said. "Here it comes. Cover your ears, everyone. We'll have five seconds."

She pressed one of the pearly teeth. It started to tick. As the train rattled by outside, Granny dived across the floor and covered her head. The other prisoners did the same.

The door flew open, a twisted, buckled mess. Shepherding the coughing prisoners out of the cage, Granny pointed to the little pile of gadgets on the floor. "Grab what you can and follow me," she said.

They skirted the outside of the cavern, staying close to the wall. Then, as they crept along behind trucks and piles of crates, a harsh siren suddenly sounded three short blasts, and a change came over the chamber. Everything stopped. Trucks, workers, everything. Nothing could be heard but the regular *clang, clang, clang,* as Proonefinger stepped onto the gantry. All eyes turned to him.

"It has come to my attention," he snapped, "that there are spies in the complex. My moment of personal triumph is due in less than five minutes. I want those spies caught before then. If not," his fat finger swept the room, "then each and every one of you will pay dearly. That is all!" And with that, he swept away.

Boilersuited guards began to comb the area, poking into every corner. Laura and the others exchanged anxious looks, but not Peabody. She turned to The Mind. "Have you got a hearing aid?" she whispered.

The Mind shook his head. "Not me. Never had any trouble with my hearing!"

"She means *her* hearing aid, dummy!"

Laura hissed. They searched their pockets.

"Is this it, Gran?" Laura whispered, holding up a small plastic item.

"Yes, dear. And you can give me that hair slide too." Peabody clipped the hair grip to the underside of a metal stair and pressed a tiny switch. A red stone began to flash faintly.

"It's a homing beacon," Peabody explained. "It may not work down here, but if it does, the Major will know what to do!"

"What about the hearing aid?" The Mind whispered. "Ah!" Peabody wagged her finger mysteriously.

One of the electric buggies passed

nearby. Peabody dashed out. "Going our way?" she asked, and with an expert throw, flipped the astonished driver from his seat.

"All aboard the Skylark!" Peabody sang, as Laura and the others piled onto the trucks.

"But these things crawl along!" The Mind wailed.

Peabody held up the hearing aid. "That's where this little gizmo comes in!" she said slapping it with a flourish onto the side of the buggy. "It's an electro-magnetic supercharger. Doubles the power of any engine", She flattened the drive pedal, and with a squealing of wheels, and a whiff of burning rubber, the buggy shot away.

As they raced across the floor, they heard distant shouting. Then they heard Proonefinger screaming from the gallery,

"GET THEM!!"

The children cowered as bullets ricochetted off the metalwork above and behind them. White-coats scattered as Peabody threw the cart this way and that.

Visored boilersuits scrambled towards the ray-gun tanks. Peabody swung the buggy round and hurtled straight towards them.

"Look out!" Laura yelled. "We're going to – "

But they didn't crash. At the very last millisecond, Peabody slammed on the brake, and twisted the steering wheel. The buggy slewed sideways, and slid, howling along the floor. The rear trucks swept across, gathering speed like a whiplash.

The laser trucks fell like nine-pins, smashed by the skidding trucks.

"Fools! Fools!" Proonefinger raged. "They're getting away!"

The cart disappeared behind some stacked crates. Above them, Peabody could see the overhead carrier track.

"Take over, would you, dear?" she yelled to The Mind. "I have to pop out!" And with that, she leapt upwards,

and disappeared. The Mind had no time to think. He just drove wildly, skidding all over the floor, leaving a trail of White-coats and Boilersuits in his wake. *"IDIOTS! IMBECILES!* Must I do everything myself!?"

Proonefinger was practically foaming at the mouth, as he hopped down the stairs, and waddled across the chamber floor like a furious blancmange.

"Where's Granny gone?!" Laura yelled.

"I don't know!" The Mind yelled back. "She just told me to drive!"

"Well *drive* then!"

"I *am!*" The Mind screamed.

"Yes, but you're not looking where

you're *GOING!!!*"

Laura's eyes went wide. The Mind
spun round - just in time to see a stack of
oil drums looming over them.

 "*AAAAAAAARGH*!" he
howled. "JUMP!"

With a tremendous
rumbling crash, the drums fell and burst.
Oil splattered all over the advancing
Boilersuits. Helplessly, they slithered and
skidded and fell. More rushed to help, but
they fell too. Then more came and fell
over *them*.

Unfortunately, Peabody's friends were faring no better. Slip-slap-sliding around, they finally struggled to their feet...and found themselves face to face with the furious Doctor Proonefinger.

"Where is she?" he growled, vibrating with rage. "WHERE IS PEABODY?!"

"Here I am!" said a voice behind him. Whipping round, Proonefinger tried to focus on the shadow the hurtled towards him. Peabody dropped like a cat from the overhead track. For a moment, Proonefinger was too surprised to move. Then he snatched up a fallen laser-gun.

"So, Peabody," he purred. "Finally I have you right where I want you!"

"Oi, Fish-face!" a voice cried. "Say cheese!" As Proonefinger glared round, The Mind lifted Peabody's torch and pressed one of the buttons he had pressed earlier. The bright white flash of the camera mode caught Proonefinger right between the eyes. Blinded for a moment, he staggered back, dropping the gun. It was all

Peabody needed. Grabbing a passing
hook from the overhead track, she
attached it to Proonefinger's coat.

"Going up!" she said.
Proonefinger's mouth formed an
astonished "O" as he was whisked off his
feet. Squealing with frustration and fury,
the evil leader was carried
away.

*"GET ME DOWN! GET
ME DOWN,
YOU NUMSKULLS!"*
he howled to his cronies
below.

"Come on, everyone!"
Peabody shouted. "Time
we were going!"

In the mess and
confusion, Peabody's team
managed to scramble to
the lift. The guards were
too busy trying to get Proonefinger down
to worry about them.

As the doors closed, The Mind saw the

clock. ZERO MINUS TWO, it said.

"Mrs P?" he yelled. "What about the countdown? We have to stop that rocket!"

"Oh, don't worry, dear," Peabody said calmly. "I've taken care of all that!"

Granny's hair-slide beacon had worked. Outside Wildwoods house, the Major had been busy. The park was sealed off, helicopters were circling, and police and army units posted at every exit. Searchlights sliced through the dark. When several shadowy figures came running out of the back door of the house, the beams picked them out and soldiers leapt from the bushes, armed and ready for anything.

"Leave them!" the Major bellowed through a megaphone. "They're ours!"

Peabody and the children ran over to him. "Hello, Major, dear," Granny said. "I'm glad you're here - there are some people I'd love you to meet. Ah! Here they are now!"

The Major looked. Wildwoods House was like a saucepan boiling over. People in white coats and boilersuits were pouring out of doors, windows, cellars and attics.

"It's total P.A.N.I.C. in there!" Laura grinned.

"All right, Sergeant," the Major said. "Round them up!"

The miserable remnants of Proonefinger's private army were herded into vans to be taken away. Laura noticed how ordinary the Boilersuits looked without their visors.

"Jolly well done, Peabody's team," the Major was saying. "Splendid job!"

The children glowed with pride.

91

"No sign of Proonefinger, sir," a young officer said. "Looks as if he's slipped through the net again!"

"Pity," said Peabody. "He'll miss all the fireworks!"

"What fireworks?" the Major asked.

Suddenly there was a quaking and rumbling under their feet. Moments later, the Helter Skelter began to tear itself from the ground. Flames ballooned all around it.

Everyone covered their eyes as a blast of hot air and leaves rushed past them, and the black and orange rocket rose,

bathing Wildwoods in an
eerie red glow, as it
shot into the sky.
"Gran?" Laura
wailed, as the spot of
gold dwindled in the night.
"You said you'd fixed it!"
"But I have," Peabody said. "As I went
past the rocket on that hook, I dropped in
our packed lunch."
The Mind gasped. "What was in it?"
"Ohhhh, sandwiches..."
"Yes..."
"Apples..."
"Yes..."
"And a few of my home-made scones!!"
They all looked up. After the noise of
the rocket, Wildwoods was unnaturally
still. Then the sky suddenly burst into a
thousand points of light, glowing orange,
then red, then white. Almost at once
another starburst lit the night.
"There's another one!" The Mind
shouted. "And another! And two more!

93

Wow!"

The Major turned to Peabody. "One thing I still can't fathom, old girl, is this: how did all those kidnapped scientists suddenly appear at railway stations in the middle of nowhere?"

"That's how, Major," Laura yelled, pointing.

High above them, a shape was illuminated by the exploding rocket. It was some sort of airship, with train wheels slung underneath, and was disappearing over the trees at enormous speed, with a helicopter in hot pursuit. Had they been equipped with telescopes, they might have seen the big moon face that peered out of the cabin window, as Doctor Proonefinger watched his dream fall in dazzling sparks from the night sky.

"I'll be back, Peabody, don't worry," he swore. "You haven't heard the last of me!"

Back on the ground, Granny turned to the children. "Well, my dears. I think that's all over. Major, dear. Do you think you could give us a lift back to Pelsham?"

* * *

A few weeks later, Laura's mum returned. Laura and The Mind ran down to meet her, Granny Smith followed wearing her usual beige skirt and cardigan.

"Don't hug me too hard!" Mum said. "I'm covered in midge bites!"

"So? How was your trip?" Laura demanded. "Was it dead exciting?"

"Actually, no!" Mum said. "The sound man caught some bug as soon as we got here, and the weather turned nasty, and the aeroplane broke down. So all in all it was a bit of a dead loss!"

"Never mind, Mum. Better luck next time!"

"What about you?" Mum whispered. "You didn't get too bored out here, did you?"

Laura and The Mind looked at each other. "Oh, it had its livelier moments," Laura said. "Didn't it, Gran?"

"Oh yes, my dears," said O. A. Peabody. "It had its livelier moments!"

THE END